James Stevenson

GREENWILLOW BOOKS

New York

For LIZ

Library of Congress Cataloging in Publication Data

Stevenson, James, (date)   Worse than Willy!
Summary: Complaining to Grandpa that their new baby
brother is no fun, Mary Ann and Louie are surprised
to hear that Grandpa's baby brother was the same way.
[1. Babies—Fiction.   2. Brothers and sisters—
Fiction] I. Title.   PZ7.S84748Wn 1984
[E]   83-14201   ISBN 0-688-02596-X
ISBN 0-688-02597-8 (lib. bdg.)

"How's that new baby brother of yours?" said Grandpa.
"Willy?" said Louie. "No fun."
"Not cute," said Mary Ann.
"All he can do is eat and sleep," said Louie.
"Or cry," said Mary Ann.

"That bad, eh?" said Grandpa.
"Your parents must feel awful."
"No," said Louie. *"They* think Willy's cute."
"They think he's smart and fun," said
Mary Ann. "They love to play with him."
"I'll be darned," said Grandpa. "Sounds
just like the way it was with *my* baby
brother Wainwright!"
"But Uncle Wainey is so nice!" said Louie.
"Uncle Wainey is so much fun!"
said Mary Ann.

"Wainey was not nice *or* fun," said Grandpa. "He was terrible!"

"Terrible?" said Louie.

"Yes indeed," said Grandpa. "But my *parents* thought he was the greatest baby in the world!

They showed him to everybody. Personally, I couldn't see what the fuss was about.

When Wainey went to bed,
there was always a big to-do.

But when *I* went to bed . . .

If I sang a song, nobody listened.

But if Wainey even *gurgled* . . .

I tried to be nice to him."

"He blamed me for everything.

He wrecked my toys.

He annoyed me night and . . .

day."

"It was the night of the great storm.
There was a howling gale . . . rain . . . flood . . .

The whole town was going past our window.

Suddenly, a passing pig knocked
me out of the window.

I called to Wainey, but
he had disappeared."

"Our house got smaller and smaller.

Suddenly, a ship came by and threw me a life preserver."

"That's what I thought
until I saw who was on the ship . . .

seventeen hideous pirates and a trained octopus!

The octopus grabbed me.

I thought it was all over . . . when suddenly a voice cried out.

It was Wainey, with one end of our papa's red suspenders tied around his waist!

Wainey jeered at the pirates.

They all ran at him.

When the pirates got near, Wainey went bouncing into the air
and the pirates hit the mast.

'You're next!' yelled Wainey at the octopus. The octopus let
me go, and tried to run away. But Wainey caught him,

tied him up, and

put him next to the pile of pirates.

Then we made our escape.

We snapped right back home!"